Tiny Garden of Words

S Afrose

Ukiyoto Publishing

All global publishing rights are held by

Ukiyoto Publishing

Published in 2023

Content Copyright © S Afrose
Pictures copyright
© to the rightful owners (downloaded, source-google)
ISBN 9789360168094

*All rights reserved.
No part of this publication may be reproduced,
transmitted, or stored in a retrieval system, in any
form by any means, electronic, mechanical,
photocopying, recording or otherwise, without the
prior permission of the publisher.*

The moral rights of the authors have been asserted.

*This is a work of fiction. Names, characters,
businesses, places, events, locales, and incidents are
either the products of the author's imagination or
used in a fictitious manner. Any resemblance to
actual persons, living or dead, or actual events is
purely coincidental.*

*This book is sold subject to the condition that it shall
not by way of trade or otherwise, be lent, resold,
hired out or otherwise circulated, without the
publisher's prior consent, in any form of binding or
cover other than that in which it is published.*

www.ukiyoto.com

To all the little to younger ones

Acknowledgement

Thank You so much dear Almighty, for being my best supporter and friend, always. Thanks a lot my dear friends and readers, and dear all children for yours' beautiful smile.

From Author Desk

S Afrose

Dhaka, Bangladesh, 15th Feb'23.

..

About the Book

"Tiny Garden of Words" is a book, containing so many beautiful artistic writes. As for example-Mother loves all, Siblings, Dear School, Friendship, Hobby etc.

With each write, there's the gist; within few words.

Those are so helpful and meaningful for any child (whether little or younger one).

Hope they will love and enjoy each of those ones, heartfully.

Contents

We	1
Mother Loves All	3
Father Doesn't Express	4
Siblings	5
Grandparents	6
Dear Uncle	7
Dear Aunt	8
Dear School	9
Respect Your Teacher	10
Try To Use Time Properly	11
Friendship	12
Eat Healthy	13
It's Your Study Time	14
Hobby	15
Outing	16
Prayer	17
Truthful	18
Take Some Rest	19

Be Kind	**20**
Feel Sorry	**21**
Share Your Love	**22**
Don't Be Upset	**23**
It's Time to Go to Bed	**24**
Early In the Morning	**25**
Little Children	**26**
About the Author	*27*

We

We sing,
We dance,
We talk,
Without any sense.

You know,
We know.
We are little children.
What can we do?

You help.
We can't.
Because,
We love to play.

But we know,

We are,

A Beautiful family.

Beloved Family!

"The Beloved Family."

Mother Loves All

Mother loves all,
Unconditionally.
Sometimes rebukes,
For a valid reason.

We must feel,
Her each word.
Mother is the best,
I love you Mom.

" Love, your Mother."

Father Doesn't Express

Father doesn't express,
His love and emotions.
He is doing his best,
For earning each of the penny.

Father also loves all.
But he is too much busy,
To make the strong base,
Of dear family.

" Love, your Father."

Siblings

We are here,
Brothers- sisters,
Siblings.

We fight,
With each other;
Still we love.

We know,
We are connected by blood.
But heart's connection is the best, at last.

"Siblings- great pleasure to be here with you, all."

Grandparents

Our Grandparents.
They live with us.
They love us.

We also love them.
We also respect them.
They are the grand pool.

" Love and respect your dear grandparents."

Dear Uncle

Dear uncle!
We love you.
Come, to play with us.

Dear uncle!
We know,
You also love us.

Together,
We will make,
The train of games.

" Make a beautiful connection with your uncle."

Dear Aunt

Dear aunt!
How are you?
Why, looking so sad?

I don't like this face.
Come on here,
Give your smile.

Let's read this book.
So beautiful.
Please, cheer up.

" Love for the Aunt."

Dear School

Dear school,
I love my school.
I love to go there.

There, I have my friends,
My dear teachers.
They love me so much.

" Go to school regularly and love the school."

Respect Your Teacher

Respect your teachers.
They are your parents.
To show, to guide you,
What is right or wrong?

Respect them.
Don't worry.
They also love you,
Though sometimes, they act as angry birds.

" Love and respect your teachers."

Try To Use Time Properly

Try to use properly,
Your time.
It will help to make,
Desired rhyme.

Time runs,
Without any pause.
You can hold that,
Only by the glamour of your deeds.

" Value, your time."

Friendship

Play with your friends.
Don't quarrel.
Take it easily.
Reflection of your dream.

Be the best.
You must show your love.
You must share your feelings.
Friendship, a precious bonding.

" Be the best friend."

Eat Healthy

Don't misuse,
Your foods.
Eat healthy,
That's good.

Health is the prime fact.
Trace this state.
You will know,
Eating timely, for the best feedback.

" Balanced diet, for being a healthy one."

It's Your Study Time

Hello dear one, don't forget.
It's your study time.
Go to your reading table,
To read and write.

You must know.
Without studying,
You can't aware of,
So many things.

Education is the Backbone,
For anyone to hold on,
The motion of life.
Just remind this part.

" Study, with your heart ❤."

Hobby

It's your desired part.
Your hobby!
Whether reading, painting, drawing,
Gardening or travelling...

Whatever-
Still your hobby.
It's essential,
To cheer up mind.

"Nourish your hobby with love."

Outing

Outing,
Is a great turning point.
To refresh all minds.

We must,
Make our time,
For making the Outing dear.

" Outing is a good trend."

Prayer

Don't forget your role.
Almighty can see anything.
Pray to Almighty.
Prayer is the best way,
To find peace,
Overall.

"Prayer, the best way to find peace."

Truthful

Always try,
To support,
The truthful site.

Lie!
It also tries,
To hold that place.

But remember,
Be honest,
To your heart and mind.

That will help,
To shower,
Drops of peace.

"Trust yourself to be honest always."

Take Some Rest

When mind will stuck,
In a jinx;
Try to open,
Vault of righteous arts.

Take some rest.
Then can find out,
The desired essence,
Of that cascade.

" Take a break, to refresh mind."

Be Kind

Be the owner of a beautiful mind.
Be the owner of a lovely heart.

Be kind,
You will be fine.

Empathy.
It's your pride.

Be Kind

Wear crown of mankind.
Be careful for the memento of human being.

" Kindness, to be the harmonic crest."

Feel Sorry

Don't be boastful.

Feel sorry.

Say sorry.

If you think,

You have made this mistake,

Then accept this.

That will help you,

To be the wonderful person.

" Saying sorry is fine."

Share Your Love

Share your love,
With all.
Don't hate those,
Who live on the road.

They are also human beings.
May be the line of social status.
But remind this fact dear,
Shower your love towards the world.

" Love all the people, without any rift."

Don't Be Upset

Dear one!
What's wrong?
Don't be upset.
Be happy always.

Ups- downs,
Life's Reel.
Don't forget this.
Just withstand, with it.

" Accept all sites of life."

It's Time to Go to Bed

Sleeping time!
In the night,
Don't be late,
To go to the bed.

Your body also seeks,
Some sort of rest.
You must believe this,
Don't forget.

" Sound sleep for the youthful vibe."

Early In the Morning

Wake up,
Early in the morning.
Don't you know?
Morning is the best time,
To refresh the body and mind.

So dear,
Keep it in the mind.
Wake up early,
Enjoy the serene breeze.

" Early morning is here to welcome you."

Little Children

Little children,
You, all are;
Like butterflies.

All of you want to fly,
To enjoy,
Dear lives.

It's obvious.
We will enjoy
Each part of our lives.

" Little children are angels."

About the Author

S Afrose

Author S Afrose (Sabiha Afrose, from Bangladesh) has made her writing realm from the past 2 years. She has enjoyed each part of her writing. She tries to say the hidden word or emotion, by her words; with the glamour of poetry. Her writes have been published in magazines and anthologies.

Published author of poetry books-Thanks Dear God, Poetic Essence, Reflection of Mind, Glittering Hopes, Angels Smile, Artistic Muse. Educational achievements-B Pharm, M Pharm from Jahangirnagar University, BD.

Contact-afrosewritings@outlook.com

www.ingramcontent.com/pod-product-compliance
Lightning Source LLC
LaVergne TN
LVHW041222080526
838199LV00082B/2058